Presented to

_____

From

_____

on this Date

_____

For my loving family and many incredible friends, especially Lane, Heidi,
Julee, Noel, Verge, my godchildren, and of course, Mom and Queenie.
A very special "thank you" to my dear and talented friends, Susan, Jeannie
and everyone at the Farmhouse Studio, and all the good folks
at Lang Books who "make it happen."

Mark

To Mark, and everyone at Lang who worked so hard on this book.
A special dedication to my wonderful studio staff for all their hard work,
and my precious family and friends.

Susan

Text by Mark Kimball Moulton
Illustrations by Susan Winget
©Copyright 2003
All Rights Reserved. Printed in the U.S.A.

Published by Lang Books
A Division of R. A. Lang Card Company, Ltd.
514 Wells Street • Delafield, WI 53018
800.262.2611 • www.lang.com

10 9 8 7 6 5 4 3
ISBN: 0-7412-1623-x

The Secret Santa of Olde Stonington

Written by

Mark Kimball Moulton

Illustrated by

Susan Winget

LANG BOOKS
DELAFIELD, WISCONSIN 53018

Nestled on a windswept coastline,
up old New England way,
lies the village of Olde Stonington
with her protected bay.

A small but thriving seaport
since the 18th century,
she welcomes friends and wayfarers
with hospitality.

Quaint shoppes with flower boxes line
her narrow, cobbled streets,
tempting wide-eyed visitors with varied,
charming treats.

Tidy, clapboard houses
perch upon her rolling hills.
A large, white church sits on her green,
devoid of fancy frills.

Tall, many-masted schooners
and immense seafaring ships,
moor near her humble fishing boats
'tween cross Atlantic trips.

The good folks of Olde Stonington
know one another well,
and call upon each other
now and then for just a spell.

Now this tale that you're about to hear
is one that's been passed down
for many generations
in this lovely coastal town.

'Tis 'bout a very special man—
a *"mystery,"* some say—
who visited Olde Stonington
one chilly, winter's day.

The year had been a trying one,
the weather, dry and hot.
The crops had withered in the fields,
which fared poor for the pot.

The sea had fared no better
and for days on days untold,
exhausted fishermen returned
with little in their holds.

The maple trees had shed their leaves—
the autumn nearly gone—
and winter's fast approach
would leave folks little to live on.

The work seemed near interminable,
though coins were far and few,
and arrangements for the winter months
still left so much to do.

Old fences needed mending,
weathered houses needed paint,
so folks in town worked day and night
'til they felt tired and faint.

But as the season fast progressed,
it looked assured to all
their chores would not be finished
fore the snow was sure to fall.

And though the words were never voiced
by townsfolk, it was clear—
there wouldn't be much left
to honor Christmas with this year.

Good parents fell into their beds,
disheartened every night,
and prayed that some small miracle
would save them from their plight...

They yearned to find an extra pence
with which to buy a toy,
or find the time to make a gift
to bring their children joy.
        Still...
they mustered their resources
in that "old New England" way—
put noses to the grindstone
and worked harder everyday.

On the outskirts of Olde Stonington,
just over Parker Hill,
lived a family by the name of Cooke
who ran the Olde Bay Mill.

The Cooke's house needed siding
as the wind would whistle through,
so Mr. Cooke began replacing
old boards with brand-new.

The task was long and arduous
and not progressing fast –
each struggle up the ladder,
that much harder than the last.
        You see…
although Cooke was a strong man,
his young wife was sick in bed,
so it fell upon his shoulders
to make sure their boys were fed.

Each morning he'd rise early,
long before the cock would crow,
to wake his boys and feed them
and then off to school they'd go.

He'd tend his farm and grain mill
and his wife, as best he could,
while struggling with house repairs
'fore cold set in for good.

Now Mr. Cooke was known to be
precise and very neat,
but as he worked, he threw old boards
in piles around his feet.

He had no time to stack them
or to haul the boards away,
so the ground became more littered
with the passing of each day.

One exceptionally cold morning
as our friend was mending lath,
he spied an old, stout, bearded man
come strolling down the path.

To Cooke, he looked familiar –
there was something 'bout his smile –
that twinkle in his eyes
and how he whistled all the while.

But Cooke could not quite place him—
perhaps he'd seen him at the mill?
Or maybe he had met him
at the General Mercantile.

His demeanor was infectious though,
and Mr. Cooke called out;
  "Welcome, friend, but watch your step.
  I've left scrap wood about."

"Good day, kind sir, and thank you!
But I wonder, may I ask—
What plans have you for that old wood
when finished with your task?"

"Why, none at all," called Mr. Cooke,
I think it's seen its day.
You're welcome to it, if you'd like.
It's only in my way."

"Oh, I can find a use for it,"
remarked the little man.
"If you don't mind, I'll help myself.
I'll take all that I can!"

So whistling, he set to work–
he opened up a sack,
and gathered all the wood he could
and slung it o'er his back.

His manner seemed familiar,
but good Cooke could not recall,
just where he'd seen the little man
or if they'd met at all.

Then with a jaunty little wave,
a *"thank you"* and a wink,
the merry man was on his way
and vanished in a blink!

Mr. Cooke began to chuckle
as he set to work once more,
indebted to his little friend
for helping with that chore.

Yet, there was something 'bout that man,
perhaps his cheerful ways,
that lightened good Cooke's heavy load
and made him smile for days.

Now farther down
the winding path
was Widow Bristol's house—
a red saltbox
with matching barn
that held her pigs and cows.

The widow'd lost her husband
early on that year –
a sickness took him suddenly
and left her ill-prepared.

She'd struggled through spring planting
with her oxen and her plow –
with fortitude she'd grown a crop
that scant sustained her now.

She'd kept her sense of humor, though,
and spiritual beliefs,
determined that she'd make her way
and rise above her grief.

A principled, strong woman,
she was full of pride, 'tis true.
So when her old house needed paint
she knew what she must do.

She gathered her last pennies
and she hobbled to the store –
bought several cans of rich, red paint
and set about her chore.

'Twas then the merry, little man came
whistling her way,
and stopped beside her garden gate
that chilly autumn day.

"Yoo-hoo, good Widow Bristol!"
the old man hailed her from the road.
"May I offer my assistance
to help paint your quaint abode?"

"Oh, dear me," answered the widow,
"you are very kind, indeed,
but I have no resources left
to pay you for your deed."

The merry little fellow nodded,
winked, then tipped his hat.
"Twould give an old man pleasure
just to help you out with that!"

"But perhaps, dear Widow Bristol,
if there's paint left when we're done,
I might procure a tiny bit.
I do have use for some."

Tears filled the weary woman's eyes
and one streamed down her cheek.
"Of course – you may have all you need,
all the rich, red paint you seek."

And so the man took off his coat,
rolled up his linen sleeves.
While Widow painted from the ground,
he painted 'round the eaves.

And when the job was finished,
she invited her friend in,
to share a bite of turkey pie
and warm, cornbread muffins.

They talked for several hours,
but when the parlor clock
struck eight,
   he tipped his hat
and took his leave—
   said it was getting late.

He carried all the paint cans
in his rumpled gunny sack,
looking like a peddler
with his wares upon his back.

The widow stepped out on her porch
and watched him stroll away,
thankful for the life she had
and friend she'd made that day.

And in the winter's darkness,
the man lit a long clay pipe,
then whistled softly
as he disappeared
on down the pike.

Several other families
were visited that year,
reporting of the bearded man
who always brought good cheer.

He worked repairing fences
or would help clear out a barn,
and all he'd take for payment
was small scraps of wood or yarn.

Each family gave this same account;
he whistled all the while –
then slung his bag upon his back
and left them with a smile.

The weeks soon passed and winter came, some say the worst in years.
Snow drifted over windowsills, *the winds blew cold and fierce!*

The good folks of Olde Stonington stayed tucked within their homes,
and watched the winter lash the sea and whip the waves to foam.

Their days were spent productively, though storms raged out-of-doors.
As Winter held his mighty grip, folks struggled with their chores.

Everyone worked hard to keep
their families warm and fed–
while boys helped chop the firewood,
young girls helped bake the bread.

And several times throughout the day,
the livestock needed tending.
Sewing, cooking, clearing snow–
the work was never-ending.

And then, before they knew it,
Christmas Eve dawned bright and clear,
and there had been no time at all
for Christmas gifts that year.

Sad parents watched their children
as they went about their way,
knowing there would be no gifts
when they woke Christmas Day.

But still they were determined—
they would make the yuletide bright,
so they worked harder all that day
preparing for that night.

They tucked fresh sprigs of holly
on the mantle o'er the fire—
placed candles on their Christmas trees—
dressed in their best attire.

Cooke called on Widow Bristol
in his one-horse open sleigh,
and asked if she would join with them
to celebrate this day.

His wife was feeling better,
after all these months, at last,
and they'd be honored if she'd come—
they'd planned a fine repast.

She said she'd be delighted if she wasn't in the way.
He told her that she'd grace their home and helped her in his sleigh.

They supped on succulent roast goose
and the Widow's fresh cornbread.
Then gathered by the crackling fire
to hear the Bible read.

Later in the evening,
as they put their boys to bed,
the Cookes sat down beside them
and affectionately said;

*"You know how much we love you
and we'd give you all we had,
but there is something we must say
that makes us awfully sad.*

*This past year has been trying
and tomorrow, when you wake,
we have no gifts to offer you,
which makes our tired hearts break."*

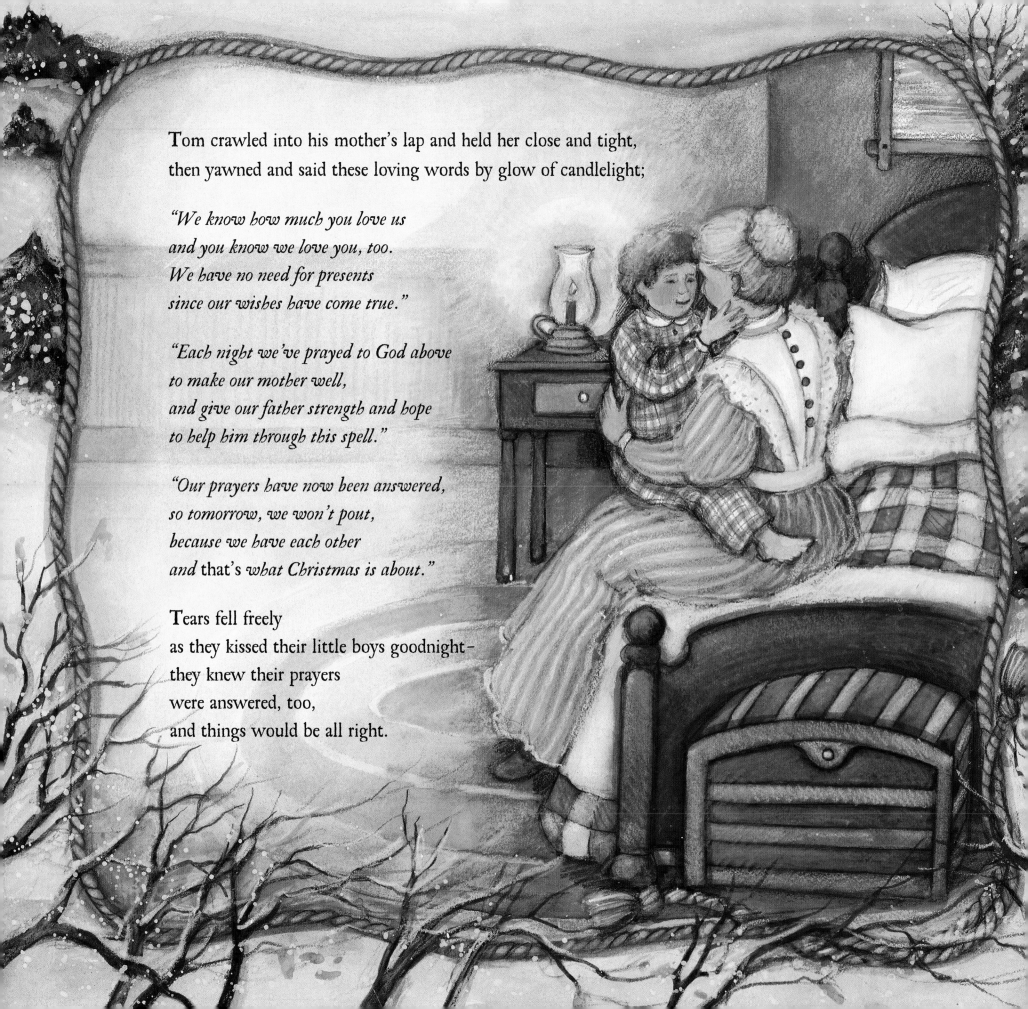

Tom crawled into his mother's lap and held her close and tight,
then yawned and said these loving words by glow of candlelight;

"We know how much you love us
and you know we love you, too.
We have no need for presents
since our wishes have come true."

"Each night we've prayed to God above
to make our mother well,
and give our father strength and hope
to help him through this spell."

"Our prayers have now been answered,
so tomorrow, we won't pout,
because we have each other
and that's what Christmas is about."

Tears fell freely
as they kissed their little boys goodnight—
they knew their prayers
were answered, too,
and things would be all right.

And as the evening settled,
soft and peaceful and serene,
the sounds of church bells reached them
from the distant village green.

Christmas morning dawned in splendor – a crisp, clear, sunny day.
The trees were draped with icicles...sun glistened on the bay.

All through the town of Stonington, bright laughter filled the air,
as children woke that morning to find presents everywhere!

There were dolls enough for every girl made from old cloth and thread,
and spinning tops for all the boys, painted a rich, dark red!

And horses set on hand-carved wheels, pulled by a length of yarn,
each painted to resemble those in every family's barn!

No one knew where they were from – those gifts that brought such joy –
but all the town was grateful, every parent, girl and boy.

It still remains a mystery who brought those gifts that day.
Some say it was by magic, some say Santa in his sleigh.

But one fact they agree upon – is late that night, it seems,
everyone in Stonington heard whistling in their dreams!

To this day, in lovely Stonington,
some townsfolk still report,
they hear a cheerful little tune
that whistles 'round that port.

And some will even tell you
that they've seen a bearded gent,
who disappears while whistling,
so happy and content.

Of course, there are those skeptics
who will frown and gruffly say,
there never was a "whistling man"
who visited that day.

But those who've seen this merry man
or heard his whistled tunes,
see "life" as being *magical*,
like summer's eve in June.

So if you hear a whistled tune
drift to you Christmas Eve,
remember that old merry man
and let yourself believe!

The End

Other Books to Collect by
Storyteller Mark Kimball Moulton
• • •
Everyday Angels

The Night at Humpback Bridge

Caleb's Lighthouse

A Snowman Named Just Bob

Miss Fiona's Stupendous Pumpkin Pies

Reindeer Moon

One Enchanted Evening

A Cricket's Carol

Teddy's Friendship Quilt

The Traveler's Gift

The Visit

Twisted Sistahs